'IN THE BEGINNING,' SAID GREAT-AUNT JANE

HELEN BRADLEY

JONATHAN CAPE THIRTY BEDFORD SQUARE LONDON

To Helen Bradley—
who
in spite
of industrial dark
saw Jonah
in Alexandra Park,
Cosmos,
Creation, the flood
in Lees, and
controlling
all the local rain,
God
in a Springhead lane—
then
among the
spectrum trees
looking through
the youngest eyes,
fixed—
a rainbow,
in Oldham's skies.

with kindest regards John Stafford, 1974.

by the same author
AND MISS CARTER WORE PINK
MISS CARTER CAME WITH US

FIRST PUBLISHED 1975
TEXT AND ILLUSTRATIONS © 1975 BY HELEN BRADLEY

JONATHAN CAPE LTD, 30 BEDFORD SQUARE, LONDON WCI

ISBN 0 224 01149 9

PRINTED IN GREAT BRITAIN
BY W. S. COWELL LIMITED, IPSWICH

IT ALL BEGAN LONG AGO WHEN GEORGE AND I WERE VERY YOUNG. GEORGE WAS MY young brother and we lived in a village called Lees. There was Grandma, Aunt Mary (the eldest Aunt), then Aunt Frances, and Aunt Charlotte (the youngest Aunt). She was very pretty: Mother, Aunt Frances and Aunt Mary had dark brown hair, but Aunt Charlotte's was the colour of honey and it curled. There was Father, of course, but somehow we didn't count him. We saw so little of him because he had to leave early to attend to business and often George and I would be in bed when he got back at night; and even on Sundays he had to see to the horses because in those days there were no cars or big delivery-vans. So Father remained in the background when we were very young.

Grandma and the Aunts lived quite near, and on bread-baking days Aunt Mary would come early to help get the dough rising and out of the oven in time for our afternoon walk. In the mornings George and I did our lessons round the kitchen table but at two o'clock Grandma would call "Are you ready?", and Mother would get us into our coats, put on her hat, and then we were ready when the Aunts had collected Miss Carter (who wore Pink). If Mrs Maitland wasn't feeling ill, she came also, bringing Dear Emily, her daughter, and away we would go along Spring Lane to the Cemetery. There we met more friends; they were Grandma's really. There was Mary Ellen, who died because she was tired of toiling with the kitchen stove; and there was Florrie, John Sam'el's wife. Mother said she was the worst gossip she'd ever known; so the Aunts, Miss Carter, Mrs Maitland and Emily had to get all their bits of news told before they met her, or everything would be all over Lees by tea-time. Miss Carter had two topics of conversation, her clothes and Mr Taylor (the Bank Manager)—and, of course (I've nearly forgotten) the Queen. She was always much discussed. Miss Carter took in one of the new magazines called *The Queen*, and in it were snippets of news about what the Queen wore, and what she ate, and the latest in sleeves and hats. It was all so interesting and exciting everyone would sit in a knot in the middle of Spring Lane discussing how last summer's dresses could be made to look like the Queen's.

On Tuesday afternoons we all went to visit Great-Aunt Jane, who lived in a large, dark, stone house up Springhead. Her rooms were dark and gloomy. Her curtains were dark-red plush with bobbles down the edge; her tables were covered in plush and so was the mantelpiece. Her walls were very dark and covered with pictures; many of them were of battles, of castles being stormed and men and horses being shot and lying dead. I did not like them.

Great-Aunt Jane told the most beautiful stories about God. "In the beginning," she always began her stories. "In the beginning, when God was young and living in foreign parts he had a shed, and there was always a lot of trouble and it hampered him. He so badly wanted to get rid of some of the Void." "What is the Void?" we asked Great-Aunt Jane. "The Void," she said, "was like thick, dark-blue velvet; but, of course, God, sitting in his shed with all that darkness around him, felt he couldn't get on. What with the troubles and the Void, he decided to make some Stars which he lit with matches and scattered about in the Void. 'Well,' he said, 'that is a bit better. I have more light.' But it wasn't enough, so he sat on his shed roof and thought for a long time. At last he made a bigger Star with a round, bright face which he polished with Brasso, and threw it into the Void amongst the Stars, but this one was big and beautiful. Not only did it give him daylight but it warmed him too and he was delighted. He laughed with joy. 'You are very good,' he said, 'I shall call you Sun.' And he had the morning and the evening that gave him time to make more things, and time to rest and sleep, and God was very happy." "What did he do next," we asked. "Well," said Great-Aunt Jane, "I'll tell you next week, because I'm going to get my hat and coat on and walk with you as far as Joe Wroe's. I must order some meat for tomorrow."

Joe Wroe sold very good meat. He reared fierce little bulls up on the moors and drove them down to his back yard and the place where he killed them. Mother and even Aunt Mary, who was very brave, didn't like passing his gate when they knew there were bulls inside, because sometimes one got out and

We looked forward to Tuesday afternoons with delight and were always eager to be off to Springhead to listen to Great-Aunt Jane telling another episode of the doings of God; but, alas, she fell asleep. Mother said, "Hush, she will soon wake—it is only a little cat-nap."

3

away it went, frightening people so that they had to run into shops and houses out of its way. But Joe Wroe's meat was very good. On Tuesdays Mother and Grandma always ordered their meat for the weekend so that Joe's boy could deliver it in his pony-trap. Miss Carter usually walked on towards Lees with the Aunts. She preferred to buy her meat in the market, saying Joe Wroe was rather dear. Mother thought her mean about food. She stinted when it came to buying the best, yet would give the earth for her clothes in Manchester; another thing Mother didn't like about her was she didn't like children.

I used to hope Miss Carter would marry Mr Taylor because I wanted to be a bridesmaid. I wanted to look like the beautiful Queen of Sheba and wear a long, green, watered-silk dress, and I began to think about the beautiful Queen of Sheba and how badly she wanted to see Solomon. She had heard all about him and how handsome he was and what a wonderful job he was making of his own country. She had plenty of money and jewels but nobody to help her with the drains or the building of new towns. So she gathered together her men, camels and money, and, making sure her green, watered-silk dress and crown were tied up in a laundry-bag, set off to find him. In a little while she saw a beautiful place with workmen still building. "My," she said, "that's beautiful. It's just like Manchester Town Hall," She quickly changed into her green, watered-silk dress, did up her hair with pins and popped on her crown. Then she walked along a red carpet to where Solomon was waiting. He certainly was a fine man and very handsome. He was doing a good job with his drains, but he had God to help him because God was living quite near and was one of the best builders that could be got. "Oh, oh," said the Queen, "I must try and get God to help me." Solomon gave her a lot of advice which she put down in her notebook, but she couldn't really think deeply because of the noise. Solomon had hundreds of wives and they all seemed to have babies which cried a lot, to say nothing of the children. There were swarms of them. So when she had found out what she wanted to know from Solomon she packed away her green, watered-silk dress and her crown and set off back to her own rather poor country. "At least", she said, "it will be nice to get home away from all that noise." If only we could get Miss Carter married to Mr Taylor I would ask Mother if I could have my bridesmaid's dress made just like the Queen of Sheba's and I would walk behind Miss Carter and be good and wear my little crown and carry some flowers.

Aunt Mary only knew the Queen of Sheba story; but Great-Aunt Jane knew lots of stories about God, and when we went to see her on Tuesday afternoons we were always anxious to know what he was doing next. "Well," said Great-Aunt Jane, "God was doing very well. He had Night and Day but he hadn't anything else. So he made some more star mixture and fashioned it into little flowers. 'Oh,' he said, 'aren't they lovely?' There were Forget-Me-Nots and Poppies, and 'You,' he said, holding up a bunch of tiny flowers, 'you are beautiful. I shall call you Daisies.' And he scattered them over the Void, but they died. He sat on the roof of his shed and thought and thought. 'I'll make a great big star but I won't light it.' So he did, and he planted it with his flowers and threw it into the Void and it blossomed and became a beautiful place. He next filled it with birds, animals and fishes; also some people, who he loved so much that he removed and went to live near them."

Then Great-Aunt Jane said, "Guess what? God's come to live up Springhead. The people he was living with in those foreign parts became very troublesome and were always fighting so he thought he'd look at Oldham and Manchester and lots of places in Yorkshire. He's got that shed on the moors not far from Harts Head Pike and judging from all the barking I've heard he's taken in all the lost dogs." "Well," said Grandma, who was listening, "perhaps we shall get some better weather. God's been used to lots of hot sun." And God, looking out of his windows, wondered how he'd come to make such a bleak place. It was certainly very damp on the moors and what bit of the sun he'd seen looked dirty and tarnished. So the next morning he was ready with a big safety-pin fastened to a long string. He climbed on to his roof and hooked the Sun out of the sky saying, "Sun, you've got very dusty and

Grandma loved Aspidistras. She wiped their leaves with milk and gave them tea to drink, because, she said, it did them good.

tarnished. It must be the smoke from the mills. I'll give you a good rub up with Brasso." And he polished the Sun until it glowed with light and warmth. Then before the people were ready to go to work God hurled it back again, and the people rejoiced in its warmth and light; and Mother and the Aunts and Miss Carter brought out their muslins and leghorn hats and everyone was happy, so happy, to walk in the warm sunshine. Mr Taylor, meeting them, very nearly proposed to Miss Carter right in the middle of Spring Lane.

But God was still puzzled about the rain. "I know what I'll do. I'll dig a hole and fit a stop tap." So he dug a hole and tested his stop tap and it worked, so he decided to set off for Manchester. "Well," he said looking at the beautiful morning, "I don't think it's wise to leave nothing but hot sunny weather. They do need a little rain." So he opened the stop tap and off he went. He quite enjoyed Manchester, but when he was just about to take the train to Bradford he got caught in a downpour. My goodness, it did rain; and he heard a voice which was Grandma's calling to him as she stood watching the rain through her new bay window. "God," she called, "don't you think it's time you came back and turned the tap off." And God set off back quickly. "It's still raining, Grandma. We can't go out in this. What shall we do?" "Well," said Grandma, "I shall have to ask David Thomas to get two men from the County End Mill and go and see what God is about." And there he was, prodding about with a piece of iron, wet through, and with a lot of wet, bedraggled dogs looking at him. "Hey, God," said David Thomas, "we've come to help you. Can't you find the stop tap?" "I was sure it was about here, but for the life of me I can't find it," said God, still prodding. Just then one of David Thomas's men put his clog in a hole and the stop tap was found. The rain took itself off, and God, rummaging in one of his drawers for a clean, dry shirt, found a beautiful strip of the finest silk. It was so light a puff of wind took it away and it made a lovely arch over the Bank Top Mill. It was a Rainbow, so away we went with Mother, the Aunts and the dogs, Gyp and Barney, for a walk before tea.

God found that he'd hampered himself somewhat with all the lost dogs. He thought when he made the dogs and cats that they would be good companions for the people, but he found that lots of people didn't care for their pets; and it saddened him. It also gave him far too much to do. One day he saw a little old lady walking up the back lane so he came down his hillside and waited for her. "Missus," he said, "I wonder if you could spare me a little time each day. I've got to go away and I haven't anyone to come in and feed the dogs. Aren't you little Mrs Winterbottom from one of the cottages down Milking Green?" "So I am," she said. "Let me know when you're off on your holidays and I'll come up." And little Mrs Winterbottom not only fed his dogs but she took it upon herself to "do" for him, and when he was at home she saw to it that he had a good plain dinner every day because he was so very good.

Usually Grandma took George and I and the dogs down Milking Green once a week to David Thomas's garden to buy cabbages and carrots, and if we stood and looked through a gate we could see God's shed away up on the hillside. Before he came I used to be very afraid of going home down the back lane from Great-Aunt Jane's because George said there was a Thing that lived on the moors near Harts Head Pike. It was called a Baycow and George said he could hear it coming nearer and nearer because it had heard us. It was a dreadful Thing and it bit people and it could even climb on to the top of trams. It said "Ha-Ha-Ha-Ha", and however quietly we walked, I was sure I heard it. Oh, Great-Aunt Jane, how I love you for asking God to come and live near to us. Since he came it's gone. I think it must have gone off towards Mossley.

Of course, there was my Dream that all the grass had died—at least it had turned blue and the sky was dark and the Void came back to the Earth and God was very upset because he'd heard rumours of trouble. Our poor King was very ill and our peaceful happy days seemed to be ending. And God stood on the roof of his shed and wept. "Oh, my beautiful Earth and my beautiful people. Just when we were so happy." And he got so upset he gave himself a headache; and while he wasn't looking fire came down.

5

But Grandma said, "Don't worry. We'll all go to the fields beyond Hopkin Mill." And there was Great-Aunt Jane and all the people of Lees. So we sat down and listened to Great-Aunt Jane, and her stories were so beautiful we forgot the Day of Judgment. And when God heard her gentle voice he became calmer and sat and listened and, looking down, saw the Sun. So he picked it up and popped it back in the sky and its warmth and light turned the grass green again and the Buttercups and flowers shook themselves and got their colour back. God blew all the fires out and told the people to rejoice and go their ways for all would be well. George and I were very hungry, so for a special treat Mother said we could have Fish and Chips for our tea.

Once I ate too much tea, and it gave me a nightmare! "Oh, Grandma," I cried, "what shall we do if the Flood comes to Lees." "Why, my love," she said, "we've all got good kitchen tables, we'll just up-end them and pretend they're real boats and sail around the Square in them. It would be rather fun. There's the big table in the woodshed that will do for Fanny (the horse)." And so when the Flood did come we all set sail on our kitchen tables. There was Mr and Mrs Smith, having their tea under an umbrella, because Mr Smith always had to have his tea at five o'clock on the dot whatever happened, and we all bowed to the Hope-Ainsworths, who floated past on their red sofa. "Oh my," laughed Aunt Mary, "won't it get damp."

The summer passed and when September came we all went to see how Grandpa was getting along at Blackpool. Our week's holiday was like a dream. We loved Grandpa and the Enchanted Garden and the sea and golden sands; but Father had to see to our business, so back home we came. But there was always Oldham Market to look forward to, and the walk back through the park. Mother couldn't understand why George and I always wanted to go home that way. "It must be the ducks they like," she said, but it wasn't. Grandma had told us the story of Jonah and the Whale and I felt sure that the black lump in the middle of the park lake was the whale and I was anxious to get back and see if it had moved. I was sure it had. One day getting near to Christmas we saw the strangest sight. There was Jonah's Whale weeping big tears and Jonah standing there in all his best clothes. "Why, Jonah," said Grandma, "I'm so glad to see you. Do come back with us for tea." But Jonah said he couldn't, he had to go to Egypt to feed his people; so alas we had to leave them and as we walked along we could hear the poor Whale sobbing.

A few days before Christmas, whilst the snow was clean and crisp, everyone, including Miss Carter, Mrs Maitland and Emily, set out to gather ivy to take up to Great-Aunt Jane, as well as our small gifts for her, in case the weather became too bad to get up the hill. And there, up near Harts Head Pike, stood God's shed, quiet and peaceful in the deep snow. We all hoped that God would stay with us for a long time.

At the end of *this* story are Grandma's flowers: flowers to remind us of God, Great-Aunt Jane, David Thomas, Grandpa and our beloved Enchanted Garden, and all those stories from our childhood. We were all so happy, and the happiness is there like a golden cloud.

"IN THE beginning," said Great-Aunt Jane, "God was young and lived in foreign parts called 'the Void'. The Void was very dark, just like blue velvet. God lived in a shed but he wasn't happy because it was so dark. 'I am living always at Night,' he said. 'I want Day.' So he made a mixture in an old barrel, rolled it into balls and lit them with his matches. They gave out a beautiful white light. 'Why,' he said, 'I'll call you Stars.' But still they didn't give him Day. So he made a very big star with a bright yellow face which he polished with Brasso until it shone. Then he threw it from the highest point in the Void. It disappeared but soon it peeped over the rim and its light and warmth delighted him. 'You are great and shall be called Sun.' He laughed and was well pleased."

"That is enough now," said Great-Aunt Jane, "it is time for you to go home."

GRANDMA, Mother, George and I, with the Aunts and Miss Carter (who wore Pink), had walked up the hill to Springhead where Great-Aunt Jane lived. We asked her to tell us more of her story, "Well," she said, "God got tired of looking at the Sun and Stars. He now had Day so that he could see to work, and Night in which to rest. But his days were long so he decided to make small things. He made a leaf, then a petal. He liked the petal so much he made lots more and joined them together in bunches. 'Oh, you beautiful things!' and he laughed with delight, 'I shall call you Daisies.' Then he made Buttercups and Forget-Me-Nots and the lovely Scarlet Poppy and scattered them about the Void, but, alas, they died. 'Well, this won't do,' said God, 'they need a home.' So he made another star, planted it with all the flowers, and sent it into the Void. The flowers grew and made the star beautiful. 'Well, well,' he said, 'now I've got Earth!'"

"GOD liked the Earth with all its flowers so much," said Great-Aunt Jane, "that he rebuilt his shed on it. Soon he saw that his beautiful Earth was getting overgrown and thought he'd better do something about it. So he made all kinds of animals—elephants, horses, cows and geese, because they liked to eat grass, and lots of little pigs to turn the soil over. He liked dogs and cats—big ones and little ones—but people he hadn't thought about until he saw how lonely some of the animals were—they needed love. So then he made a rough-looking girl called Eve and a fine lad called Adam." Soon after Great-Aunt Jane told us this story we all went to Blackpool, and when we were picnicking on the sandhills, I was sure we saw them. Aunt Frances said to Mother, "Jane, I don't like that wild-looking pair." "No," said Mother, "we shall have to find somewhere else." Mr. Taylor (the Bank Manager) took Miss Carter's basket and found us another nice place to have our picnic tea.

9

WHEN WE were back in Lees we forgot about seeing Adam and Eve and it wasn't until we went again to Grandpa's that we remembered them. On our first day everybody got up early to go to the farm for milk, which would be still warm from the cows. We walked first through the Enchanted Garden—how fresh and dewy the flowers were—but before we came to the stile leading to the farm we saw that someone had lit a fire. "Goodness," said Mother, "if it isn't the pair we met on the sandhills: it's Adam and Eve with their dear baby." Eve held him out to Mother. "We've got a little him," she said. He was very new and very beautiful but poor Mrs Maitland wept. "Oh," she cried, "if poor Samuel hadn't died, I might have had a little boy." Miss Carter wouldn't look. She didn't like new babies.

Grandma, the Aunts, Mother, George and I, Miss Carter and, of course, the dogs, Gyp and Barney, had been to Great-Aunt Jane's Birthday Party. The day hadn't been as nice as our usual visits because we wore our Best Clothes and we had to sit still. We longed for her to tell us a story about God. She only had time to tell us a bit, but it was good news. "Well," she said, "God has come to live in a shed not far from Harts Head Pike." He had come to see what Lees, Oldham and Manchester were like but he was finding it rather cold and damp. Great-Aunt Jane hadn't seen him but she'd heard that Mrs Winterbottom was going to help him, and all the lost dogs had heard about his coming and had gone to live with him. How glad George and I were to know that God had come to live near us—we should not be afraid again of the Thing that lived on the moors. As we walked down to Lees we looked at God's shed and saw a light come on. God was at home.

HELEN BRADLEY

Now that George and I had found where God lived we badly wanted to see it in the daytime. We asked Grandma to take us for a walk down Milking Green to David Thomas's garden. "Well, children," said Grandma, "get your hats on," and away we went. David Thomas was in his garden smoking his pipe, and, whilst he and Grandma talked, George and I looked at God's house—and lo and behold, there were lots of dogs waiting outside. There were all sorts, big dogs and little dogs. Two were actually sitting on the roof! As we watched, a little old lady in a red shawl went up the steep path. "Grandma," we cried, "look at all those dogs!" "Goodness me, whatever next," said Grandma. "It's all right," said David Thomas, "they're only waiting for their dinner. I believe God's gone away and Mrs Winterbottom's on her way to feed them. She's taken on something; looking after that lot. I see I shall have to lend a hand," said David Thomas, and Grandma laughed and laughed.

GOD was nicely settled in his shed up Springhead, but he was dismayed at the dullness of the Sun. So he got up very early, hooked it out of the sky with a safety-pin on the end of a piece of string, and gave it a good polish with Brasso. Then he put it back again. Oh, we had a glorious week of beautiful sunshine then! God thought next that he'd dig a hole and fit a stop tap so that he could regulate the rain because it wasn't good to have hot, dry weather all the time. Then he decided to have a look at Manchester and before going thought he'd better turn the tap on. Oh, my, it did rain. "God," said Grandma, "I wish you'd come back and turn the stop tap off." The rain didn't stop, so Grandma asked David Thomas to take two men from the County End Mill to see what God was about. They found him looking perplexed and very wet. "Hey God," David Thomas cried, "have you lost the stop tap?" Just then one of the men found it by catching his clog in the hole, and God promptly turned the tap off.

13

WE REALLY had a *lot* of rain. Grandma said it was because God kept going away and there was nobody to turn the tap off, but of course, it being early Spring, we couldn't expect good weather yet. One day we got caught in a downpour in Milking Green. The lady who lived at the corner asked us into her house, but the rain didn't last long. "Look, Mother," I said, "look at the sky: there's a beautiful rainbow." "Yes, dear," said Mother, "when God was rummaging in one of his drawers he found a beautiful strip of finest silk. It was so light a puff of wind took it away and it made a lovely arch in the sky. Now God always sends a rainbow to tell us the rain will soon go. But *look* at George, he's walking in that puddle: he'll be wet through."

AFTER SO much rain the weather improved at Easter, when a sad thing happened. Poor Mrs Clark lost both her sons. They were killed in a mine. Grandma said "Let us all take daffodils up to their grave in Greenacres Cemetery." It was a lovely day as we walked up the hillside where we met poor Mrs Clark and her youngest son's widow, Ruth. "How are you, dear Mrs Clark?" asked Grandma. "I shall not be lonely now," said Mrs Clark. "Look who's come to live with me – our dear Ruth." "Why, that is nice," said Grandma, "it's just like the lovely story of Ruth and Naomi, isn't it? Ruth who came to her mother-in-law Naomi and said, 'Where you go, I go also.'" Mrs Clark and Ruth came to live in Lees and later Ruth married again and had three little boys, so Mrs Clark's life became full and happy again.

"WELL," said Aunt Mary, "the Queen of Sheba was very lovely. She wore a dress of green, watered-silk and had lots of jewels and gold; but her Palaces were poor places, with bad drains and plumbing. The Queen thought something had better be done. She heard about King Solomon and what a fine man he was, so she thought she'd better count out some gold and jewels to offer him in return for some help. One fine day she gathered together her camels, her men and her bags of treasure. She put her green, watered-silk dress and her crown in a bag and set off. She came within sight of a beautiful place. 'My,' she said, 'it's just like Manchester Town Hall,' so she changed into her Best Dress, did her hair up with pins and put on her crown. Then she went to meet Solomon. He thought her lovely and she thought him handsome. With him was God, busy with rolls of plans, for being a great builder, God was helping Solomon with his drains."

THERE was great excitement when Mother, Grandma, the Aunts and Miss Carter took George and me on a trip to London. It was a beautiful place. Not only did the King and Queen and all their children live there, but it was so light and clean we were sure God must have a little house there somewhere. Although we all wore our Best Clothes, which had the latest puff sleeves, when we got to Regent Street all the smart people were wearing quite different styles. Grandma said they were all Lords and Ladies; but we forgot our dowdiness when two smart bays trotted close by us and we saw in the Landau the beautiful Princess Mary dressed in shell-pink lace. She saw us and smiled. The shops were more wonderful than anything in Manchester, especially the shop opposite where we were standing. It was filled with rose soap and rose perfume. "Look," said Grandma, "I'm sure that's James and Emily Forsyte with their son, Soames; but how sad his wife, Irene, looks. She is walking towards us in that lovely grey dress."

SOON after our London trip was the day of the Tea for poor children. The people of Lees baked and made potted meat and jellies, and when the day came, Mother, the Aunts, Miss Carter and lots more ladies made a most delicious Tea. The children and mothers arrived in wagonettes, then a lorry brought the Parson, Mr Green (the new Curate), some more men, and a lady to play the Harmonium, and the Service began. One poor little girl cried—she wanted her Tea: she'd had no dinner. At one Tea, Great-Aunt Jane said, God felt sorry for the children having to wait so long, so he propped the two halves of Jacob's ladder against each end of a pink cloud. "Hey, children," he said, "up you go." And up they trooped to the Happy Land, which was like a big bouncy Feather Bed. What a good time they had: God kept them on the move. "Down you go carefully." When they got to the bottom the people were singing "There is a Happy Land, Far, Far Away". The children laughed, and shouted "We've been, we've been," and, at last, Tea was ready.

"OH, MY beautiful Earth. Oh, my beautiful people," God cried out. He had been called hither and thither trying to settle troubles, and there were so many they made him tired. There wasn't even time to see to all the lost dogs and cats whom he loved so. He climbed on to the roof of his shed and listened to the rumble of discontent. He held out his right hand. "Please," he said, "Give thought to me. I made you, and I made you so beautiful; and all the animals and birds I made, and they are beautiful. I gave you all love, yet you are without it," and a tear ran down his cheek. He wept and was so sad it gave him a headache. The Sun, seeing him so sad, came out of the sky so there was nothing but dark-blue Void, and out of it came fire which descended on the Earth. "Oh my Beautiful World, what will become of you?" All the lost dogs heard his cry and howled, and everyone heard their long howl and they were afraid for they knew now that God was very angry. That night was still, dark and very hot and only that afternoon Great-Aunt Jane and Grandma felt that God was very unhappy at the way things were going. The King was very ill and our peaceful, happy way of life seemed to be ending; so, instead of a story, she read the last few verses of the Old Testament: "And the Earth shall burn and all that do wickedly shall be as ashes—they shall leave neither root nor stock."

ALTHOUGH it was fine and should have been a lovely day, it was dark and foreboding; so we went to Grandma, and found her looking at her garden. The grass had died; at least it had turned blue. "Dear me," said Grandma, "Everyone get ready and bring the dogs and cats and tell Father to get Fanny (the horse) and we'll all go to the fields beyond Hopkin Mill." We hadn't gone far before the Sun went out of the sky and the Void came down and it was like dark-blue velvet and the people of Lees came out of their houses and followed Grandma to the fields. Sure enough, the grass had turned blue and all the flowers and trees had turned white with fright, and round and about there was burning. Then Grandma said, "Come, we will sit here and Great-Aunt Jane and I will tell you stories for, alas, I'm afraid this is the morning of the Day of Judgment."

"OH," SAID God. "Oh dear," he said. He had quietened down somewhat after being so upset and wearied with his troubles, and, as he sat on the roof of his shed he heard the gentle voice of Great-Aunt Jane telling her stories about God and his great goodness as everybody sat in the gloom about Hopkin Mill surrounded by the Void, which was very dark, like dark-blue velvet. "Oh," said God again. "Oh dear me, this won't do. I've given myself a headache being so sad." And he took one look at the fires that had started and felt despair. "Oh dear," he said again, "what will my people think of me?" And as he sat looking disconsolately at the Sun which had come out of the sky, he heard again the voice of Great-Aunt Jane talking to all the people of Lees. "Why," said God, "she's telling them the story of Ruth and Naomi." "And Ruth, pretty young widowed Ruth," said Great-Aunt Jane, "went up to her mother-in-law and took her hand saying, 'where you go, dear, I go also', and that was good, kind love." And God, listening, remembered Ruth and Naomi and their sorrows. Then he thought he'd better do something so he blew out the fires, hooked the Sun to a safety-pin and flung it back in the sky. Then God got off his roof and began to feel better and all the lost dogs came and begged for their dinner. "Well, well," said God, "come along all of you and we'll see what Mrs Winterbottom has left for us."

21

WHILST God was feeding his dogs, Great-Aunt Jane told stories so beautiful that all the people of Lees forgot it was the Day of Judgment. They forgot the fires and God's sadness and God himself forgot his troubles as he listened to Great-Aunt Jane. Looking down from his shed he thought, "Well, they don't look such a bad-looking lot, sitting there above Hopkin Mill in all this gloom!" In no time at all the Sun was back in its right place, the grass stopped looking blue and the butter-cups shook themselves till their lovely colour came back, and the trees sent out new buds. The people sighed a great sigh of gladness and gradually drifted back to work and their homes. God said all the animals could go back to Belle Vue Zoo, except for Biddy Murphy's Tiger, which lived in Lees. *He* became so good he let Annie and Willie Murgatroyd stroke him! We were very hungry so Mother said we could have Fish and Chips for tea because we had all come through the Day of Judgment safely.

22

FOR THE past two weeks Miss Carter had been very quiet. Although the Aunts called for her she didn't answer the door. They and Mother wondered what she was up to. Eventually, when Aunt Frances called, Miss Carter greeted her saying, "I was just about to ask you to come to tea tomorrow." Tomorrow came and into Miss Carter's house went the grown-ups but, as she didn't like children, George and I had to go and play in her back yard along with Gyp and Barney. Afterwards Mother said that Miss Carter had had her sitting-room decorated and her new wallpaper was black with pink roses. She had a new carpet and everything was beautiful. Mrs Hope-Ainsworth came and was rather rude and bossy, but Dear Mr Taylor was very nice to her and got her to leave early so that the other ladies could enjoy a good gossip.

23

"THEY'RE off," called John Sam'el's wife Florrie, who was standing on a chair peeping through the blind with Martha Higginbotham, who was counting the neighbours following the Hearse. "We can't feed all that lot," said Aunt Mary, busy slicing ham. Mother wasn't thinking about the food but about Great-Uncle Tom's Sideboard. "I wonder who he's left it to," she said. Aunt Annie (who was only an Aunt by marriage), said, "Jane, you've enough furniture. I could do with that Sideboard." Just then Sarah's voice was heard from upstairs, "Everybody's making for the front gardens and I can hear a bull bellowing!" Mother, Aunt Mary and Aunt Frances rushed upstairs to see what was happening. Sure enough Joe Wroe, the Butcher, was so busy watching Great-Uncle Tom's funeral that he had forgotten to fasten his bulls in. Two were soon caught but one ran down into Lees and deterred several people who had been coming to the funeral tea, which made it easier for the Aunts. Alas, we didn't get the Sideboard.

WHEN the Autumn came we all went to Blackpool to see how Grandpa was getting along. We hadn't had our usual long Summer holiday because Father had been very busy, but we spent the lovely Autumn there. Our days were so filled with joy and sunshine that we nearly forgot God living up on that bleak, cold moor in his shed. We told Grandpa about him, and Grandpa said he would write and offer him *his* shed to have a holiday in. It was right in the middle of the Enchanted Garden and God would find it quiet and peaceful. The leaves became golden and the blackberries were big and juicy. Mother and the Aunts gathered baskets full to take back with us, along with three barrels of apples, because blackberries and apples didn't grow around Lees; it was too bleak.

SOMETIMES on Friday afternoons Mother, George and I, with Grandma, the Aunts and Miss Carter, walked through Goldwick to visit Great-Aunt Buckley. Like Great-Aunt Jane, she lived in a big, dark house and she was very strict. We usually had to sit still and be good but sometimes she would let us play in the kitchen. There was always Polly, her maid, sitting before the fire. She had a big black cat called Joe who loved to play hide-and-seek with us. Polly made delicious Parkin and George and I always had a lump before going home. This time we didn't go straight home but instead went into Oldham, to Baileys' Pot Shop because Mother had remembered just in time that tomorrow was Mrs Maitland's birthday and we had promised her a cream jug. We bought her a lovely one with pink roses all over it.

ONCE when I must have eaten too much tea I dreamed that it rained and rained until the Square in Lees was a lake with little waves. "Oh, Grandma, what shall we do?" I asked. "Well, my dear," said Grandma, "don't you remember God promised there would never be another Flood? We've just had a bad storm and the drains won't take all the water. We'll have to get our kitchen tables." We up-ended all we could get and launched them like boats. Willie Murgatroyd tied the table-cloth to the legs of their table; it made a splendid sail. And he brought his fishing-rod and fished. Mr and Mrs Smith brought their little round table and sat eating their tea, and Mrs Hope-Ainsworth and Bertie and Nellie and the dog floated along on their red sofa, which Aunt Mary said would get damp. Then the rain stopped and the water drained away: it *had* been fun.

GEORGE and I loved to walk home through the park after we'd been shopping in Oldham. Mother used to say, "It's because they like to see the ducks." But it wasn't. It was the black lump in the middle of the park lake that fascinated us. Grandma had told us the story of Jonah and the Whale, and one afternoon when we were walking by the lake I asked Grandma if a Whale could get in. "Well," she said, "if it did, it certainly couldn't get out." George and I were *sure* that the thing they called an island was really a Whale's back, and the more we looked at it the more sure we were that it had moved a bit nearer the landing-stage.

29

ONCE I dreamed that after we'd walked through the snowy park on our way home the little black island moved and the Whale's great head came out of the water near the landing-stage. To our great surprise out walked Jonah dressed in his Best Clothes. "Bless me," said Grandma, "if you aren't Jonah!" She took his hand and seemed very pleased to see him. "Now you must come back with us and have a cup of tea." "Oh Missus, I can't," he said, "I've to go and see my people." "Where are your people?" asked Grandma. "They're in Egypt," he replied. "But you can't go all that long way without your tea," said Grandma. But just then the Whale wept long and loud because it wanted Jonah to come back and stay with it.

THE SNOW came down a few days before Christmas. Grandma, the Aunts, Mother with George and me, Miss Carter and Mrs Maitland and Emily, went down Milking Green to gather ivy for Great-Aunt Jane to decorate her house. We took her our gifts also because she lived up Springhead and whilst the weather was good we thought it best to go and wish her a Happy Christmas. Walking back through the quiet lanes we heard the Church Bells ringing out that it would soon be Christmas. We were sure God was very happy for we could feel there was peace and quietness everywhere.

GRANDMA'S FLOWERS

Here are the Pale Roses you loved,
And Daisies that are so beautiful,
God's little Flowers that he loved,
Gathered with care
And painted with joy,
From a Garden of Memories.

HELEN LAYFIELD BRADLEY 1974